Sammy Saw

by Adria Klein   illustrated by Andy Rowland

MEET THE
TOOL
TEAM

Tia Tape Measure

Hank Hammer

floor section

Sammy Saw

Sophie Screwdriver

The tool team is at school.

"I have some big news,"
says Hank.

"What is it?" asks Tia.

"We are going to make the sets
for the school play," says Hank.

"Fun!" says Sophie.

"Cool!" says Tia.

"Oh, no," says Sammy.

"What's wrong, Sammy?"
asks Hank.

"I can't do it," says Sammy.
"I always make mistakes."

"Don't worry," says Hank.

"We'll help you," says Sophie.

"I'm nervous," says Sammy.
"I know I will make a mistake
and ruin the play."

"With our help, you can do anything!" says Tia.

"Come on, Sammy!" says
Sophie.

"I guess I'll try," says Sammy.

"Here's the plan, team,"
says Hank.

"Tia will measure the wood,"
says Hank.

"Great!" says Tia.

"Sophie and I will hold the wood," says Hank.

"Great!" says Sophie.

"And then Sammy will cut the wood," says Hank.

"I'll try," says Sammy.

"Let's do this!" says Hank.

"This piece is too long. We need
to cut it," says Tia.

"Are you ready, Sammy?"
asks Hank.

"I don't know," says Sammy.

"You can do it!" says Hank.

Sammy stands up straight.

"You're right. I can do this!"
he says.

Sammy saws up and down.
He is very careful.

The tools work hard to build
the sets for the play.

Sammy is no longer worried. He is having fun with his friends.

"Not too short. Not too long. Sammy, you cut everything just right!" says Tia.

"You did it, Sammy!"
says Hank.

"Thanks for helping me,"
says Sammy.

"That's what friends are for,"
says Hank.

STORY WORDS

school	measure
news	piece
mistakes	worried

Total Word Count: 252

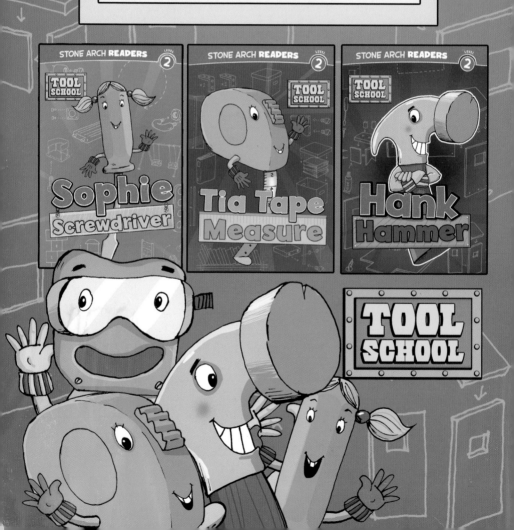

STONE ARCH READERS — LEVEL 2

TOOL SCHOOL

Sophie Screwdriver

STONE ARCH READERS — LEVEL 2

TOOL SCHOOL

Tia Tape Measure

STONE ARCH READERS — LEVEL 2

TOOL SCHOOL

Hank Hammer

TOOL SCHOOL